My Grandmother's
Cookie Jar

My Grandmother's Cookie Jar

by
Montzalee Miller

Illustrated by
Katherine Potter

PRICE STERN SLOAN, INC.

Library of Congress Cataloging-in-Publication Data

Miller, Montzalee, 1956–
  My grandmother's cookie jar.

  Summary: Grandma passes on the stories of her Indian people to her grandchild as they eat cookies
together from the cookie jar shaped like an Indian head.
  [1. Indians of North America—
Fiction. 2. Grandmothers—Fiction]
I. Potter, Katherine, ill..   II. Title.
PZ7.M63144My   1987   [Fic]   87-3146
ISBN 0-8431-1587-4

Copyright © 1987 by Montzalee Miller
Illustrations copyright © 1987 by Katherine Potter
Published by Price Stern Sloan, Inc.
360 North La Cienega Boulevard, Los Angeles, California 90048

To my parents
—M.M.

To Jocko, Joan and Roy, Alison,
Jonathan and Stephen
—K.P.

It sat at eye-level on the dark shelf in my Grandmother's kitchen, waiting for me, as it always did. The head seemed to laugh at my fear. I couldn't help but watch its face in the shadows. Was it watching me back?

I stared at it until I made myself silly with fear. Suddenly a hand touched my shoulder. I jumped and turned to see my grandmother standing quietly behind me.

Grandma smiled at me, and with a flip of the light switch, the Indian head cookie jar was stripped of its blanket of shadows. It sat silent and alone upon the shelf.

Grandma took off his headdress,
reached inside and brought out a cookie for
me. My eyes never left his painted face.
Even with the lights on, I was a little
afraid.

Then Grandma and I sat at her table, as we did each evening, and she told me a story of her Indian people of long ago. I knew her stories by heart and I loved them all. As she stroked her long, grey and black hair she told of places that seemed too wonderful to be.

Grandma's stories made me feel and see the days of old. I could smell the smoke of the open fire. The chants sung by the painted dancers filled the clear night air. I could feel the freedom of living under the starry sky.

I felt my pony under me as we raced
after buffalo. The hills around were black
with their many numbers.

I could also feel the Indians' fear of the people who took the land away. I could smell the odor of the thousands of hunted buffalo and see their bleached bones scattered across the plains.

I felt Indian pride and understood Indian honor. I longed for the ancient ways.

With each cookie there was a new adventure. Even the quiet Indian head cookie jar seemed to enjoy listening to Grandma.

Then one day Grandmother was gone.
Grandfather came to me with the
Indian head. He told me it was full. I did
not want a cookie. I was sure they would
not taste the same without Grandma's
stories to go with them.
I took the head very carefully and
looked inside. It was empty.

Grandfather put his hands on my shoulders and looked at me as if he could see all my thoughts, all my fears and all my dreams.

"The jar is full of Grandma's love and Indian spirit," he said softly.

"When you are grown and have children of your own you will put cookies in this jar. The cookies will be dusted with Grandma's love."

I stared at the jar's painted face. I did not know how I felt.

"If you tell one of Grandma's stories with each of the cookies," Grandfather went on, "then her spirit, and the spirit of those who went before her, will live on."

I looked into the eyes of the cookie jar. My fear was gone. I knew that the Indian head cookie jar and I had an important job to do.

"I will keep the spirits alive," I said firmly, just as Grandfather had. "I will tell Grandmother's stories."